THE OWL AND THE WOODPECKER

For Rebecca

THE OWL AND

FRANKLIN WATTS, INC.
845 THIRD AVENUE, NEW YORK, N.Y. 10022

© Brian Wildsmith 1971. First published 1971 by Oxford University Press. First American publication 1972 by Franklin Watts, Inc. SBN 531-01553-X. Library of Congress Catalog Card Number: 74-165476. Printed in Austria.

THE WOODPECKER

Brian Wildsmith

Once upon a time
in a forest far away
there was
a Woodpecker.

The Woodpecker lived
in a tree in which he slept all
night and worked all day.

One day, an Owl
moved into the tree
next door. He liked to
work all night and
sleep all day.

The Wood-pecker worked so hard and made so much noise dur-ing the day that his tapping woke the Owl.

"Hey, you there!" screeched the Owl. "How can I possibly sleep with all that noise going on?"

"This is *my* tree," the Wood-pecker said, "and I shall tap it as I please."

The Owl lost his temper. His screeches and hoots echoed through the forest, and animals for miles around came running to see what was the matter.

"Oh, be quiet," growled the Bear. "Woodpecker, stop tapping, and let Owl sleep. We like a peaceful life around here."

"You go right on tapping, Master Wood-pecker!" squeaked the Mouse. "Owl is always bossing and chasing us."

Angrily, the Owl swooped down on the small animals, who ran for their lives and hid in all kinds of curious places. "You big bully!" they shouted, when they were sure they were safe.

Then the Owl asked the bigger animals what he could do to stop the noise, but they all shook their heads.

"How should we know?" they said. "*You* are the wise and clever one. Perhaps you could move to another tree."

"Why should I?" snapped the Owl. "I *like* living in this tree. That noisy Woodpecker must move!"

But the Wood-pecker would not move. Day after day his noisy tapping kept the Owl awake. And day after day the Owl became more tired and more and more bad-tempered. He began to be so crotchety and rude that all the other animals decided something must be done.

So they held a meeting.
"Something must be done," said the Badger.
"Woodpecker was here first, so Owl must be the one
to leave."

"But he says he will *not* leave his tree," replied the Deer. "In that case we shall have to push down the tree, and then he will *have* to leave," said the crafty Fox.

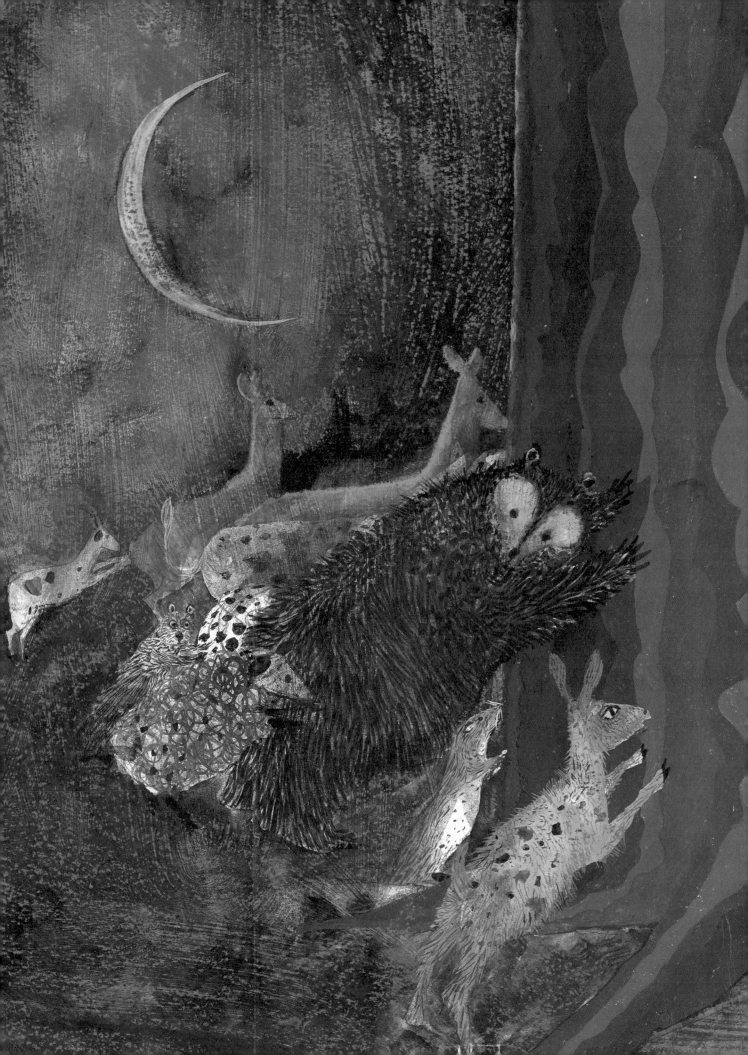

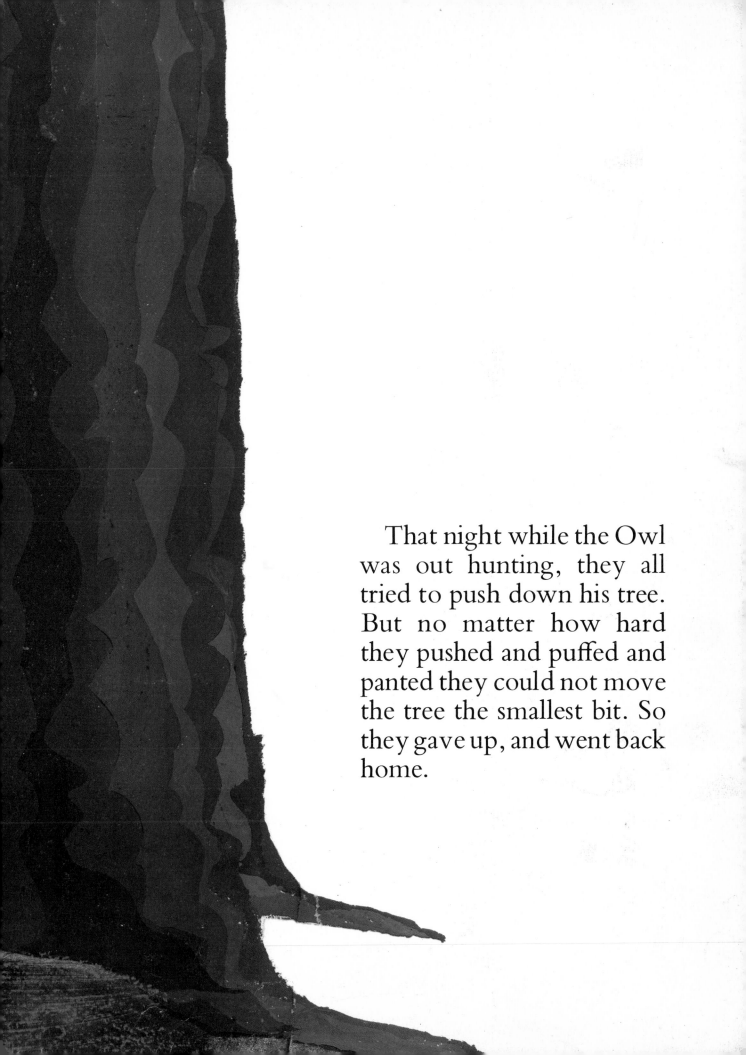

That night while the Owl was out hunting, they all tried to push down his tree. But no matter how hard they pushed and puffed and panted they could not move the tree the smallest bit. So they gave up, and went back home.

Some time later two strangers came to the forest—a pair of Beavers. They took a fancy to the Owl's tree, and started to gnaw at the trunk.

Every day they gnawed a little more, until it seemed as if they would gnaw the trunk right through.

Then one day a great storm shook the forest. The wind roared through the trees. It was so strong the Woodpecker gave up tapping, and hurried to find shelter. So for once the Owl slept in peace.

The Owl's tree began to creak and crack and groan as the wind grew more and more fierce, but the tired Owl slept soundly on.

Suddenly the Woodpecker saw the Owl's tree begin to sway and fall. At once he struggled bravely out into the storm and tapped loudly close to the Owl's ear to wake him. The Owl woke up in a fury when he heard the Woodpecker tapping on his tree. But when he realized his tree was being blown down, his anger quickly disappeared.

Together the Woodpecker
and the Owl struggled to safety just
as the tree crashed to the ground.

Then the storm died away, and the Owl thanked the
Woodpecker for saving his life. Now he was glad that the
Woodpecker had been his neighbor.

So the Owl and the Woodpecker became good friends, and the Woodpecker helped the Owl to find another tree in a quiet part of the forest, where he could sleep all day without being disturbed.

Peace and quiet returned to the forest and the Owl and the Woodpecker remained good friends all the rest of their lives.